Published in Great Britain by Brimax,
An imprint of Autumn Publishing Group
Appledram Barns, Chichester, PO20 7EQ

Published in the US by Byeway Books Inc,
Lenexa KS 66219 Tel 866.4BYEWAY
www.byewaybooks.com

Original manuscript by Myrto Nielson
Story adapted by Lynne Gibbs
Illustrated by Michalis Kountouris

Published by arrangement with NIKASBOOKS Athens-Greece

Printed in China

Dear Little Bear

Illustrated by

Michalis Kountouris

BRIMAX

More than anything, Bobby Bear wished he had a toy boat like the one that belonged to his best friend, Billy.

One day, Billy Bear said, "You can play with my boat today, Bobby. But you must give it back to me tomorrow."

"Oh, thank you!" said Bobby. "I will bring the boat to your house in the morning!"

But Bobby had so much fun playing with Billy's boat that he didn't want to give it back.

The next morning Bobby had an idea! If he didn't take the boat back to his friend as he had promised, perhaps Billy would forget about his toy. Then he could keep the boat forever!

Meanwhile, Billy waited for Bobby to return his toy boat.

As the days passed, Bobby happily played with the red and white boat.

I was right! Billy has forgotten that I still have his boat, thought Bobby.

But one morning, a visitor came to Bobby's house. "I've come to see you!" called a voice.

Oh, no – it's Billy! thought Bobby, as he quickly tried to hide the boat.

"What are you doing?" asked Billy, coming into the room.

"Um, nothing. Nothing at all," said Bobby.

"You were trying to hide my toy boat!" said Billy, crossly. "Did you think I would forget that you still had it?"

"Um… no," said Bobby. "Well, yes, yes I did!"

"I'm very sad," said Billy, taking his boat.
"I thought we were friends, but you wanted to
keep the boat more than you wanted to be
my friend."

"I'm so sorry," whispered Bobby. "I just wanted to play with your lovely red and white boat for a little while longer."

Without saying another word, Billy quietly left the room.

Bobby bowed his head in shame.
He couldn't blame his friend
for being cross.

As he walked home, Billy let out a big sigh and shook his head from side to side.

If only Bobby had asked, I would have let him keep my toy boat for as long as he wanted, thought Billy, wiping away a tear. I'm sad he didn't understand that.

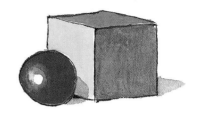

Bobby was also very upset.

"Oh, dear little bear, whatever is wrong?" asked Bobby's mother.

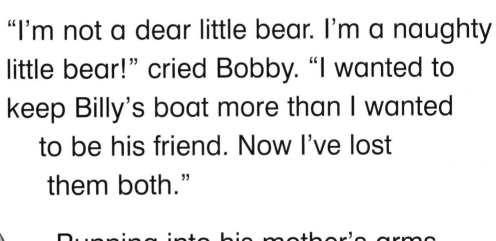

"I'm not a dear little bear. I'm a naughty little bear!" cried Bobby. "I wanted to keep Billy's boat more than I wanted to be his friend. Now I've lost them both."

Running into his mother's arms, Bobby cried until he had used up all his tears.

"Friends are far more important than toys," said Bobby's father, as the little bear sat on his knee.

"I know that now," said Bobby. "But will Billy ever forgive me?"

"I'm sure he will," smiled Bobby's father. "You must go and tell Billy that you want to be his friend much more than you ever wanted his toy boat!"

And that is what Bobby did.

"Billy has forgiven me!" said Bobby, rushing back into the house a little later. "He said that as I am such a dear little bear, I can borrow his toy boat until tomorrow!"

"Just as long as you don't forget to give it back!" said Bobby's father.

"I promise," said Bobby.

Next morning, as Bobby sat down for breakfast, he looked at the red and white toy boat.

"I shall miss playing with the boat," he said. "But I would miss playing with Billy even more! Friends are much more important than toys."

"What a dear little bear you are," smiled Bobby's father.